Season

By Raven Howell

Illustrated By Ann Pilicer

Seasons
Written by Raven Howell
Cover and Interior Illustrations by Ann Pilicer
You may find additional work at www.annpilicer.com
Published March 2023
Skippy Creek
Imprint of Jan-Carol Publishing, Inc.

ISBN: 978-1-954978-83-6
Library of Congress Control Number: 2023933669

You may contact the publisher:
Jan-Carol Publishing, Inc.
PO Box 701
Johnson City, TN 37605
publisher@jancarolpublishing.com
www.jancarolpublishing.com

Jan-Carol
Publishing, Inc

"every story needs a book"

"Innovative rhymes and the clear flow of one period into the next make the concept of seasonal change easy for young readers to grasp. With action-packed illustrations and a repeating refrain, this nature tale is sure to become a favorite read-aloud in preschool classrooms."
— Kirkus review

"This is a wonderful journey to introduce children to winter, spring, summer, and fall. I recommend this book to all parents and educators who want to help children learn about the seasons and the changes that occur in an interesting, fun, and interactive way."
— Readers' Favorite

"This picture book conveys so much in a few words, a striking element the author understands very well. The illustrations have a wonderfully 'classic' feel — stunning!"
— The Wishing Shelf

Goodbye, winter

Hello, spring!

Bye, chilled toes

Hi, green thing!

Crack, egg, crack

Sing, bird, sing!

Goodbye, winter
Hello, spring!

Goodbye, spring
Hello, summer!

Bye, ball slugger
Hi, beach bummer!

Buzz, bee, buzz
Hum, bug hummer!

Goodbye, spring
Hello, summer!

Goodbye, summer
Hello, fall!

Bye, vacation
Hi, school hall!

Hoot, owl, hoot
Your moonlit call!

Goodbye, summer
Hello, fall!

Goodbye, fall

Hello, winter!

Bye, leaf pile
Hi, ice splinter!

Blow, snow, blow
A peppermint-er!

Goodbye, fall—
We're back to winter!

CPSIA information can be obtained
at www.ICGtesting.com
Printed in the USA
JSHW040932250423
40773JS00006B/112